Ice Hockey

Trace Taylor

It is on.

This is my hockey shirt.

Here are my hockey pants.

Come and get me.

Here are my hockey gloves.

Look at this.

Here are my hockey skates.

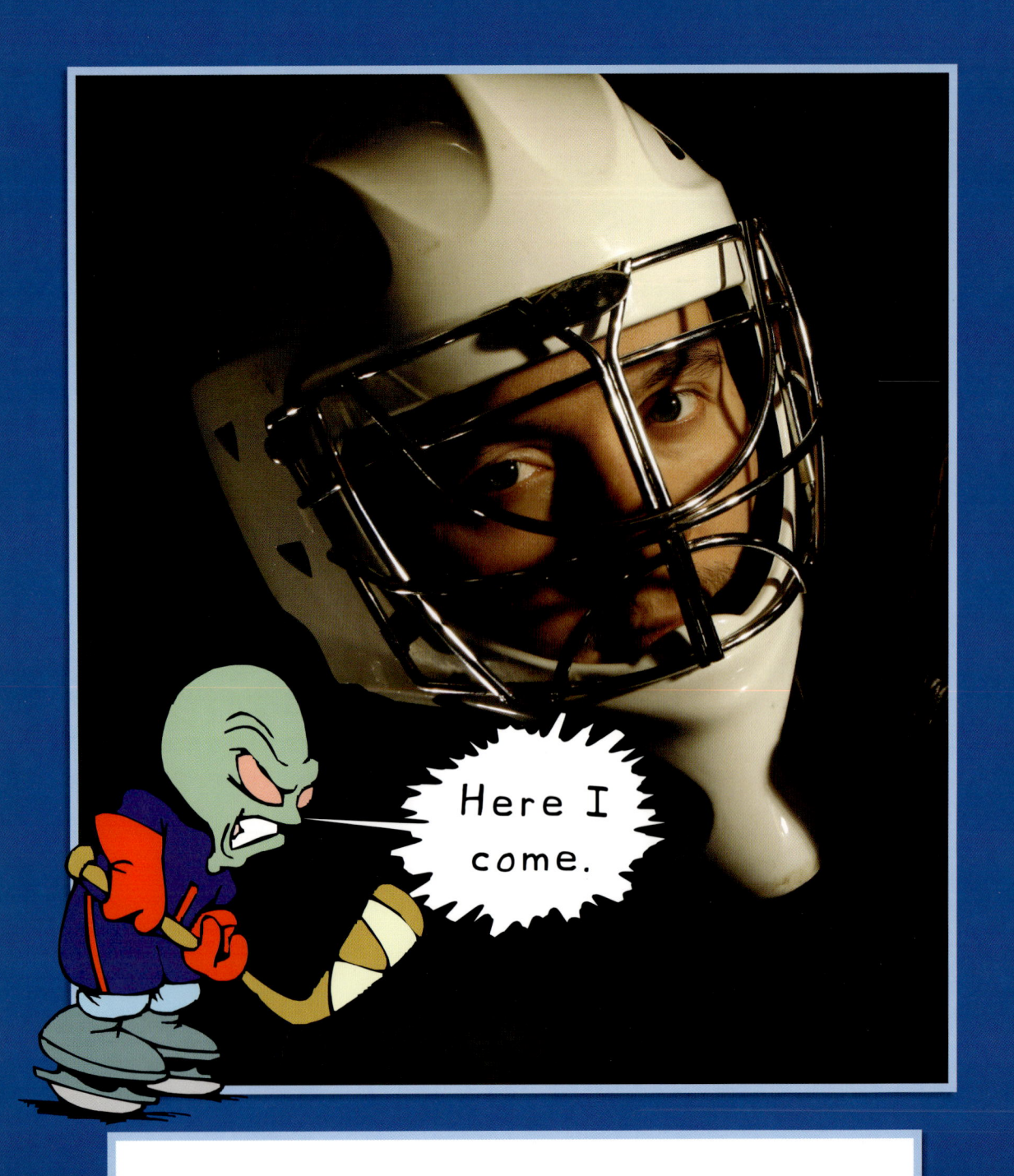

This is my hockey mask.

Here are my hockey pads.

This is my hockey stick.

This is my hockey team.

I am the big one.

This is my hockey puck.

Are you up to this?

Here is my hockey net.

I have you.

This is my hockey game.